To Rosemary
From Philip —
My very best,
'83

LONG MEG

LONG MEG

by Rosemary Minard

PICTURES BY PHILIP SMITH

PANTHEON BOOKS
NEW YORK

For Bernie
and
for my mother and father

Library of Congress Cataloging in Publication Data
Minard, Rosemary. Long Meg.
Summary: Meg, an innkeeper's daughter, as tall as the tallest man in Westminster, puts on her father's clothes and joins the British army setting out to invade France led by the King himself.   1. Boulogne-sur-Mer (France)—Siege, 1544—Juvenile fiction. [1. Boulogne-sur-Mer (France)—Siege, 1544—Fiction. 2. Henry VIII, King of England, 1491-1547—Fiction. 3. Heroines—Fiction] I. Smith, Philip, 1936- ill. II. Title.
PZ7.M6517Lo [E] 81-11103
ISBN 0-394-84888-8 AACR2
ISBN 0-394-94888-2 (lib. bdg.)

CONTENTS

I

The Inn at Westminster

LONG ago in England, when King Henry VIII ruled over the land, there lived in the town of Westminster, just outside London, a young girl named Margaret. No one ever called her Margaret, though, except maybe her mother when she was mad. To everyone else, throughout Westminster and all around the countryside, she was known quite simply as Long Meg.

And that was because she was tall. Strikingly, stunningly tall. For what had happened was this.

When Margaret was twelve, she'd started to grow. I mean *really* grow. And in less than a year she'd shot up right past her oldest brother, Will. At fourteen she was as tall as her father. And by the time she was fifteen, she was gaining on her Uncle Ben, who was so tall he had to stoop to get through doorways.

Margaret's father began to worry. "Another inch," he fretted each time he measured her against the doorjamb. And he confided to his wife, "She's got to stop this growing soon. We're almost up to the top of the door!"

But Margaret's mother only gave a little smile and said, "Never mind. She'll stop when it's time."

And she did, of course. When she was sixteen, she stopped growing as suddenly as she had started. By then, though, she was as tall as the tallest man in Westminster. And that is why everyone called her Long Meg.

Now, contrary to what you might expect, Margaret didn't mind being called Long Meg. And she didn't mind being tall, either. Not even when rude children stared and pointed and giggled. Not even when her elders gasped and said, "My, you've grown like a weed!"

In fact, she found being tall quite handy for certain things. Like seeing over other people's heads ... or reaching up to the top shelf. And it didn't hurt a bit to be as big as her brothers. For Meg could run as fast as Will, throw as far as Tom, and wrestle Jack to the ground before he could count to twenty.

Meg's father worried about that, too. " 'Tisn't proper, madam!" he said to his wife at least once every day. "Tongues are wagging about our Meg. It's a disgrace the way she runs about in breeches and wrestles with the boys.

And worst of all is her swordfighting, that infernal fencing. She's at it every spare moment, I tell you."

It was at fencing, though, that Meg really shone. With her long arms and legs, she could outthrust, outlunge, outparry, outduck, and outdodge not only Will, Tom, and Jack, but anyone else who dared to take her on—including Sir James of Castile, the most famous swordsman in Westminster and about the biggest braggart in all England.

Sir James bragged at court about his distinguished ancestors from Spain. He bragged in the shops about his satin suits from France. And he bragged at Meg's father's inn about his surpassing skill with a sword. If Meg had heard him once, she'd heard him a hundred times. Then one day she decided she'd heard enough.

"There's not a man in all England can match me with a sword," he was boasting for at least the fifth time that day just as Meg arrived with his fifth pot of ale. "Send me any and all comers," he bellowed. "I promise to make quick work of them."

Meg plunked his pot down on the table and stifled an urge to make quick work of Sir James right then and there. Instead she smiled sweetly and looked deep into his eyes.

"Indeed, sir," she cooed, as meek as she could manage, "I know of a body might be a fair match for you. And you will find him at five o'clock this very evening out walking by the windmills in St. George's Fields. He wears a blue coat and a broad-brimmed hat, and I'll warrant he would welcome your challenge."

"Touché!" cried Sir James, always eager for a chance to show off. "And," he added, jumping to his feet so that everyone could hear, "if this fine champion should be the

winner, I'll pay for his supper tonight and wait on him at table myself."

Later that afternoon, just before five, Meg stole away to the small, low rooms in the attic where she and her family lived. She pulled on a pair of her father's close-fitting breeches and slipped into an old blue coat he no longer wore. She borrowed his second-best boots and tucked her hair up tight under a broad-brimmed hat. Then she grabbed up her sword and sped away to St. George's Fields.

Sure enough, when she got there Sir James of Castile was waiting. As soon as he saw her, he strode straight up and threw down his glove.

It's a pity, thought Meg as her eyes ran over his fine silk hose and his fur-trimmed doublet, to have to mess up that nice suit of clothes.

But before she could think anymore, Sir James reached for his weapon. *"En garde!"* he shouted, and Meg pulled out her sword. The next moment the air was filled with the ringing of blade against blade.

Sir James was superb with his sword, all right, but it was clear he had met his match. Whichever way he thrust, there was Meg blocking his stroke. And her footwork was so neat and so nimble he grew dizzy just trying to keep up. So, up and down the fields they went, whacking and

banging and slicing the air until at last Meg gave Sir
James such a blow that his sword flew out of his hand.

Sir James had lost his fencing match.

That night half of Westminster must have crowded
inside the inn to watch Sir James of Castile serve the mysterious stranger who had beaten him. Still in her disguise,
Meg sat at a table all by herself right in the middle of the
room. Sir James stood behind her, gazing contemptuously
out at the crowd from under half-lowered eyelids. After

all, he was still Sir James of Castile, descended from a long line of splendid Spanish ancestors. Yet with his nose turned up and his mouth turned down and his chest stuck out as far as it would go, he looked as if he might just as well have come from a long line of bulldogs.

At last the dinner began. With a haughty flick, Sir James shook out a great linen napkin and tied it around Meg's neck.

"Humph!" he snorted and stomped off to the kitchen. And it was then his troubles went from bad to worse.

On his way back to the table he dodged to miss a lady's elbow, and Meg's pickled eels slipped off the plate and down the front of Mistress Wiggleworth's bodice. On his next trip from the kitchen he dribbled the gravy down Bartholomew Belcher's collar. And when he tried to carve the roasted pheasant, its drumstick shot off and into the lap of Friar Dominic's Sunday cassock.

All this time Meg never said a word, but ate her supper in silence while Sir James scurried back and forth, slipping and dripping and dropping his way into deeper and deeper disgrace—much to the delight and amusement of everyone who had gathered to watch.

But what with all the merriment, if anyone wondered why the mysterious stranger ate his supper with his hat on, no one bothered to ask. And if anyone mentioned that the twinkle in the stranger's eye looked just the least bit familiar, everyone else was laughing too hard at Sir James to notice. So you can imagine the squeals of surprise when at last the mysterious stranger stood up and pulled off his hat and turned out to be none other than Long Meg, the innkeeper's daughter!

And imagine Sir James's shame. He turned from pink to rose to scarlet, crimson, and purple. And from that moment on he never again bragged about his surpassing skill with a sword, he didn't have much to say about his satin suits from France, and he only mumbled now and then about his distinguished ancestors from Spain.

As for Meg, from that day on, no one in Westminster ever teased her about being tall or gossiped about her swordfighting again. The townspeople all said wasn't it wonderful the way she'd taught that upstart foreigner a thing or two about the English. And the rude children who had stared and pointed and giggled before, now followed her about the town and begged for tips on how to handle a sword.

Meg thought it was fine to be admired, but more than anything else her duel with Sir James had given her a taste of adventure—a taste that was delicious. And she yearned for more.

But about the closest Meg ever came to adventure was when she served supper at the inn. Every evening hungry soldiers crowded inside to dine. As she served their plates and filled their cups, the soldiers' stories spun and swirled in her head, and she dreamed of what it might be like if she were to go away with the king's army.

Sometimes dreams come true. But Meg knew that hers never would. Who had ever heard of a woman in the army? Much less a girl of sixteen! Besides, she had to work at her father's inn. And there was too much work for dreaming:

"Meg, dear, brush up the crumbs from around those chairs!"

"Beat that cream till it's good and thick, Meg, and mind you don't let the sauce stick!"

"Here, Meg, polish this pot till you can see your face in it!"

Day in, day out, there were the same tiresome chores—food to be cooked, beds to be made, and floors to be swept and scrubbed. And as one dull day slid into the next, the duel with Sir James slipped further and further back in Meg's memory until she scarcely thought of it at all.

Then, one night as Meg was serving supper, the dining room was buzzing with excitement. For many months there had been trouble brewing between the English and the French. The French had made friends with the Turks and the Scots, who were enemies of the English. All that day rumors of war had been flying about the town. King Henry, it was said, was planning to invade France, and that evening the soldiers could talk of nothing else.

"The king himself will lead his troops," Meg heard a man say as she leaned across his shoulder with a steaming plate of meat.

"Aye," replied his neighbor, taking a deep whiff of the Yorkshire pudding that followed. "King Harry is the noblest knight in Christendom. He marches forth to defend the honor and glory of England. 'Twill be the greatest army to leave these shores in more than a hundred years."

As Meg moved on to the next table, the talk was the same there. And at the next table. And at the next one after that. "Two hundred ships . . . thirty thousand soldiers . . . seven thousand men on horseback . . ."

Meg shut her eyes to picture the scene. She saw ships with gilded prows and silver-painted masts. She saw knights in shining armor, their horses prancing, their bright-colored banners whipping and flapping in the wind, their swords glistening at their sides.

Suddenly the memory of her duel with Sir James flooded through her like a tide. She could feel again how her arms and legs and feet had worked perfectly together. How her sword had moved with a magical life of its own. . . .

The next moment the door burst open and in marched one of the captains from the army. "By order of the king," he roared, "all men must report to their companies by midnight. We leave at dawn for France."

No one was more excited by this news than Meg. Late that night, when all the soldiers had left and she was clearing off the tables, she remembered what her Aunt Betty often said: "If you don't scale the mountain, you can't view the plain."

Now, Meg knew she wanted to view something besides the inside of that inn. There was no doubt about that.

But then she remembered that Aunt Prudy always said, "Dry bread at home is better than roast meat abroad." And for a moment she wasn't so sure.

But of all her aunts, Aunt Minnie was her favorite, and what Aunt Minnie always said was, "Nothing ventured, nothing gained."

That settled it. Meg set down her tray, took off her apron, and ran up the stairs to her room.

Quiet as a mouse, she pulled on the same close-fitting breeches she had worn to meet Sir James of Castile. She found the same blue coat her father no longer wore, and for the second time she borrowed his second-best boots. She tucked her hair up tight again under the same broad-brimmed hat, and buckled on her same trusty sword. And when she had stuck a note on her mother's pillow, she tiptoed down the stairs and out of the inn.

II

Calais

MEG stood on the dock and looked out to sea. Ships, as far as she could see—their masts bobbing up and down like sewing needles—waited for a turn to come in to shore and unload.

It felt strange to think that only six days ago she'd been home in Westminster, serving soldiers at the inn. Yet here she was today, a soldier herself, in a city called Calais—an English city on the French side of the English Channel.

How long ago it seemed that she'd slipped out of the inn and raced away into the breaking dawn. She'd headed right for the river. That was where the ships were. That was where the troops would be. Likely she'd find a way to enlist.

She'd hurried through the narrow streets of Westminster, tripping on cobblestones, almost turning an ankle, fearing each time she turned a corner that she'd run into someone she knew. Yet, except for an occasional greengrocer rattling back from market, his cart piled high with cabbages and potatoes, the town was still asleep, its streets almost deserted. Once she'd seen a familiar-looking man coming toward her and had ducked into a still-darkened doorway, holding her breath as the shadowy figure passed. At last she reached the mighty Thames, its waters silvery with the day's first light, its docks teeming with men.

Some of the men—the ships' crews—wore gorgeous

coats of green and silver-white, the king's colors. But most, like Meg, were dressed in everyday work clothes. Gray, brown, olive, dark blue, burgundy. In such a crowd she'd felt sure she would never be noticed. The river Thames was filled with ships, some moored along the wharves, some anchored farther out. In the growing light, Meg could make out bright-painted galleons and sturdy caravels. Here, a lean, low galley, its rows of upturned oars straight and even as clean-picked fish bones. There, an enormous warship, its bulk spread over the water. And,

darting in and out like waterbugs, rowboats filled with sailors and supplies hastened with the loading.

Yet one ship stood out above all the others, so huge it looked like a floating fortress. Meg could see at least six decks and too many guns to count. Banners and pennants flew from every mast. It was plain to see that this was a very special ship.

Meg inched her way into the crowd and sidled up to a boy who looked to be about her age.

"She's a mighty ship," Meg offered, careful not to sound too eager.

"Aye, that she is," replied the boy. "She's the *Great Harry,* the king's own flagship. Takes a crew of nigh onto nine hundred just to sail her," he continued, obviously glad to have someone to talk to and happy to share his knowledge. "But it'll take a sight more hands than that to man all those guns. I mean to go aboard as a gunner."

"That so?" replied Meg. Then, in a voice so cool you'd have thought she was just being polite, "And how do you mean to go aboard?"

"Nothing to it," the boy said with a shrug. "Yonder sits the commander for the king's company. Unless ye be too young or too old, sickly, or weak as a woman, he's sure to take you. . . . Zounds!" he exclaimed suddenly, looking Meg over from head to toe. "You'd not make a bad soldier yerself, tall fellow like you."

"Well, maybe," Meg replied. "Only thing is," she said to herself with a grin, "I fear the commander might find me weak as a woman. . . ."

And with a giggle she was gone.

"What's yer name, lad?" barked the company commander without looking up.

"Uh, Me . . . er, Marg . . . uh . . ."

Meg's face went white as a boiled sheet. *A name.* She had to have a man's name. She hadn't thought of that.

A moment passed. It seemed like an hour. Meg licked her lips and her mind raced. The commander looked up.

"Name, lad!" he bellowed.

"Uh . . . Long . . . er, Me . . . uh, Greg, that is. Greg Long, sir," Meg blurted, gradually recovering her wits.

But by this time the commander had leaned forward and was looking Meg up and down. Then he looked her square in the face. Meg felt as if his beady black eyes would bore a hole in her.

"Yer a tall one, y'are," he said at last, "but I'll warrant yer a young 'un yet. No beard . . . voice like a choir-boy . . . How old are ye, lad?"

"Sixteen, sir," Meg answered at once in a voice so deep she could hardly believe it was hers.

"Hmmm . . ." said the commander, and he reared back in his chair to look her over again.

Meg pulled up her shoulders and looked straight ahead and waited. . . . She hoped he couldn't hear her heart pounding.

"You'll do," he snapped at last. His chair thumped forward and in his book be wrote, "Greg Long, foot soldier, sixpence a day."

And before he looked up again, Meg had disappeared up the gangplank of the *Great Harry.*

The next days ran together in a haze of sunlight for Meg. Sunlight that caught in the gold threads of wind-filled sails. Sunlight that shattered on the sea like splintered glass. Sunlight that burned noses, parched lips, scented the salt breeze that blew in her face. July sunlight that drenched the city of Calais as the English fleet sailed into her harbor.

The *Great Harry* had been one of the first ships to arrive, and Meg had hopped ashore as soon as she could, eager to help with the unloading. Already ships were lined up against the piers. To one side was an elegant galley, the *Virgin Mary,* and farther down a bit were two big warships, the *Peter Pomegranet* and the *Mary Rose.* In the opposite direction the *Lion* and the *Sweepstake* strained at their ropes.

Sailors scrambled everywhere, lowering sails and

knotting ropes, pushing, pulling, tossing, stacking, as the great cranes hauled up an endless array of supplies from the ships' holds. Along the dock, piles of hammers, shovels, and pickaxes lay scattered about with shields, swords, helmets, whole suits of armor. Meg picked her way among them, stepping carefully so as not to upset the stacks of laundry tubs, cooking pots, and shaving basins that balanced uneasily on top of mattresses and straw pallets.

"Soldier! Lend us a hand here," came a cry from the *Great Harry.* Meg looked up just in time to catch a crate swinging down at the end of a crane. Then came a chest, more crates, kegs, casks, bags of grain, great hoops of cheese.

"Look out!" came another cry, and Meg jumped aside as barrels by the dozens bumped and rattled down the gangplank and jammed into each other on the dock.

"Make haste, soldier," bellowed the same impatient voice. "Set those barrels to rights and stack them alongside the crates."

So Meg plunged in, joined by five more soldiers who jumped down from the ship to help. And as the morning sun climbed high in the sky, Meg and her companions sorted and stacked barrels and more barrels filled with everything from nails and horseshoes to biscuits, barley, sugar, rice, dried peas and beans, candles, salt, and cider.

Suddenly from the *Lion* there came such a racket that Meg started up from her work. And what she saw made her mouth fall open, for out of the ship's hold came not barrels or shaving basins, or even swords or shields, but a stream of cows, sheep, pigs, chickens, and geese. Bawling and cackling, they plunged down the gangplanks, only to be rounded up again onshore.

" 'Tis for food," said one of the soldiers who had been helping Meg with the barrels. And he added proudly, "King Harry's men will have no need to rob the barns and hen houses of French peasants." Then, looking at Meg as if he were seeing her for the first time, he began again abruptly: "By Our Lady, lad, ye look like ye've had a dunking. No need to keep yer coat on in this blisterin' heat. Here, let me help ye out of that. . . ."

Meg stepped back in horror as the soldier reached for her top button. Not only, she realized at that moment, was her coat soaked through with sweat, but she was the only soldier stacking barrels who had not stripped to the waist!

"No . . . I . . . you see . . ."

"Fools! Knaves! Bumbling flea-brained boobies! Mind your clumsy, stumbling feet or you shall find them pacing a prison!"

Meg stopped in mid-sentence. The soldier's hand stopped in midair. Both whirled around to see the spectacle coming down the gangplank, a sight more amazing than either barrels or barnyard animals, a sight so astonishing they forgot all about the heat and Meg's coat and simply watched in wonder.

First of all, there was a man—about the fattest man that Meg had ever seen, with a belly like one of the barrels she'd spent the morning stacking. And what's more

he glowed. His beard glowed red because of the July sun, his face glowed red because he was in the midst of a temper tantrum, and his suit glowed gold because that was what it was: gold cloth embroidered all over with gold thread. Gold chains hung about his neck, and on his fingers were gold rings—some set with jewels as big as robins' eggs.

So this is the king, thought Meg, for this remarkable person could not have been anyone else. And she remembered the man at the inn who had said that the king himself would lead his army.

Yet the thing about the king that was most astonishing was not his size or his temper tantrum or even his suit of gold. What was truly amazing was that he was *in bed*. Propped up against a pile of pillows, he lay on his royal litter, raging at the poor porters who had stumbled and almost sent him tumbling into the dark sea below.

A crowd had gathered to watch the king and the commotion, and Meg worked her way up front for a better view.

"What ails the king?" she asked her new neighbor, wondering how a sick king could possibly lead an army.

" 'Tis his leg," replied the man with a sad shake of his head and a knowing glance at Meg. " 'Twas at a tourney it happened, a good many years ago. Ah, King Harry . . .

he was a sight to see in those days. The grandest knight in all the land. Entered all the lists and took all the prizes. Shattered many a lance, he did. And you should ha' seen 'im ride. Had the finest horses—barbs that could run like the wind, high-stepping Neapolitans that could turn and jump and fairly dance. Saw 'im once on a fine black Arabian. Looked like St. George in person—"

"But what about his leg?" Meg interrupted. "What happened to his leg?"

"Aye, that was a sad day, indeed. 'Twas in '36. Time and again His Majesty ran in the jousting. He seemed to have the strength of ten men that day. Then, all of a sudden, he clashed with a knight and fell from his horse and the great beast fell on him. Ever since, his leg is given to terrible swellings. Causes him no end of agony. And now that he's got so fat, he can hardly get around on it at all."

Meg watched the king for a moment. He was safely down the gangplank at last, and his porters were hauling him up and down the dock and from one ship to another. Pompous as a peacock, the king was waving his arms and shaking his fists, snorting and shouting orders. But why, Meg wondered, would a king who can't walk leave his comfortable bed in the palace for a portable cot on the dock of Calais, far away on the coast of France?

Then she had a thought—the kind of thought that

you know is so before you're even finished thinking it: King Henry had been as bored at home as she'd been. He was as sick of his stuffy life at the palace as she was of her tiresome work at the inn. She looked at the king. Fuming and fussing one minute, laughing and shouting directions the next, red in the face from so much excitement, His Majesty was having a wonderful time. He was glad he'd come.

And so, thought Meg, am I.

III

The Siege

’**T**IS a good omen. . . .”
"A sign from Heaven . . ."
"A bright beginning . . ."
Murmurs and whispers swept through the crowd as
the king's porters pushed, shoved, boosted, and heaved
their massive monarch into his saddle. His Majesty's leg
was much better. He would ride his shining black war-
horse on the road to Boulogne. It was a sure sign of good
luck.

Moments later, to a fanfare of drums and trumpets,
King Henry VIII of England led his army out of the gates
of Calais and into the French countryside. Nobles and
knights on horseback fell in behind with banners and
lances held high. Then came archers, gunners, pikemen,
and soldiers on foot. And strung out behind like a ragged

"What city is that?" asked Meg of an old soldier beside her.

" 'Tis Boulogne, lad," replied the man, "the city King Henry will capture if he has his way. But 'twill be no easy matter, you can see that for yourself."

"Aye, good father," said Meg. "That great wall yonder is as tall as a two-story house. And 'tis thick enough, I'll wager, for five soldiers to walk side by side along the top."

As they drew closer, Meg looked up and down the solid wall before her. How ever will we get through? she wondered.

"Break ranks!"

"Make camp!"

The order passed from company to company, and soldiers and workmen rushed about unloading wagons, pitching tents, staking pavilions, digging trenches, building earthworks, placing cannons, grooming horses, tending livestock. By the end of a week a small city had sprung up on the plain below Boulogne.

Boom! Baroooommmm!

The bombardment began. The great guns of the English spat fire and stones and cannonballs at the walls of Boulogne. Over and over they pounded the walls, every day for a week. Then two weeks. Three weeks. Four. And all that time from the city there was nothing but dust and flying rock and silence. Though cracked and pocked and crumbling in places, the walls of Boulogne stood fast. And so sure were they of their safety that the soldiers inside the city didn't even bother to fire back. Perhaps what the French said was true: Boulogne would never fall.

But King Henry didn't believe it.

"Send me my engineers," he bellowed, stroking his beard and limping from one side of his tent to the other. "We will devise a new plan—a plan that cannot fail."

And they did.

For two nights the army's trenchmakers crept up the hill to a spot where a giant crack zigzagged up the wall. There they dug and scraped and dug some more until the ground beneath the crack was as full of tunnels as a rabbit warren. Then they stuffed the crack and the tunnels with bombs made of stones and gunpowder and hurried back to the camp.

"Fire!" ordered the king.

Boom! Five cannons at once shot at the crack in the wall.

Baroooommmm! Baroooommmm! The wall rocked and heaved and swelled and split. Yellow spurts of flame shot out in all directions. *Whoosh!* A gust of wind slammed into

"What city is that?" asked Meg of an old soldier beside her.

" 'Tis Boulogne, lad," replied the man, "the city King Henry will capture if he has his way. But 'twill be no easy matter, you can see that for yourself."

"Aye, good father," said Meg. "That great wall yonder is as tall as a two-story house. And 'tis thick enough, I'll wager, for five soldiers to walk side by side along the top."

As they drew closer, Meg looked up and down the solid wall before her. How ever will we get through? she wondered.

"Break ranks!"

"Make camp!"

The order passed from company to company, and soldiers and workmen rushed about unloading wagons, pitching tents, staking pavilions, digging trenches, building earthworks, placing cannons, grooming horses, tending livestock. By the end of a week a small city had sprung up on the plain below Boulogne.

Boom! Barooooommmm!

The bombardment began. The great guns of the English spat fire and stones and cannonballs at the walls of Boulogne. Over and over they pounded the walls, every

stung her eyes and stuck in her nose and mouth. Her head throbbed from the bawling of cattle, the squawking of chickens, the constant pounding of drums. And with each step the raw spot on her left heel was getting worse. It was a blister coming—from the boots. Her father's second-best boots.

Toward evening, Meg was thinking about the inn—they'd be getting ready for supper now—and trying not to think about the heat and the dust and the noise and her blister and trying not to be homesick, when she came around a bend in the coastline. In the distance before her, high on a hill, a city rose up against the sky. And surrounding the city was a great stone wall.

III

The Siege

'T IS a good omen. . . ."
"A sign from Heaven . . ."
"A bright beginning . . ."

Murmurs and whispers swept through the crowd as
the king's porters pushed, shoved, boosted, and heaved
their massive monarch into his saddle. His Majesty's leg
was much better. He would ride his shining black war-
horse on the road to Boulogne. It was a sure sign of good
luck.

Moments later, to a fanfare of drums and trumpets,
King Henry VIII of England led his army out of the gates
of Calais and into the French countryside. Nobles and
knights on horseback fell in behind with banners and
lances held high. Then came archers, gunners, pikemen,
and soldiers on foot. And strung out behind like a ragged

ribbon came those who would never see battle, but were
there to see to the needs of those who would: brewers,
bakers, butchers, smiths, carpenters, armorers, masons,
trenchmakers, bricklayers, surgeons, and priests.

Heading south, the army marched along the tops of
the steep chalk cliffs that border the French coast. The
summer sun burned white in the sky, and Meg felt her
hair getting damp and heavy under her hat.

I'd give a gold piece, she thought, if I could just take
off my coat.

On every side, cannons, carts, and wagons, bake ovens
and brewing vats rumbled along behind mules, oxen, and
enormous draft horses, kicking up a curtain of dust that

the English camp, and king, soldiers, Meg—everyone—dashed for cover as blocks of stone and chunks of mortar shot into the air in a cloud of smoke and rained down the hillside.

When the dust had settled, there was a huge gap in the wall where the crack had been. For a moment there was silence. Then, *Boom! Boom! Baroooommmm!*

The air filled again with the thunder of cannon fire. Only this time it was the French. At last they had turned their guns onto the English. Suddenly the camp was a confusion of collapsing tents, rearing horses, flying splinters of barrels and carts, and soldiers running this way and that.

Boom!

A cannonball slammed into the earth not far from Meg, and she threw herself to the ground in a shower of dirt and rock and metal. Moments later she was on her feet again, wondering which way to run.

Zimmmmmmmmmm! Zimmmmmmmmmm!

Arrows whizzed just over her head. Then, *Zimmmm,* another passed, lower and so close this time she felt it almost brush her cheek. A hand reached out and grabbed her, and down she went again.

Slowly she inched her way up to see a company of French knights come galloping through the gap in the wall and race down the hillside. Armor gleaming, lances outstretched, they crashed into the line of English knights speeding forth to meet them. Then foot soldiers rushed out from all around, and Meg was swept along into the thick of the battle.

There was no time to think, only to pull out her sword and fight. Then there was no need to think. *Clang!* Her sword struck that of a Frenchman and she was back in Westminster at St. George's Fields. Her challenger was

Sir James. Her feet and sword worked like magic, and one French soldier after another saw his sword fly out of his hand and found himself a prisoner of the English.

At last there were no more French soldiers. They were running back to the city with the English hot on their heels. Meg looked about her in the lull that followed. And what she saw made her shudder. All at once she felt sick. And sad. And angry.

Men dead and wounded lay scattered about in the dirt. Here and there a great war-horse lay silent and stiff, or writhing and twitching with pain. Everywhere there was blood and suffering and death and dust and the acid smell of gunpowder.

Meg felt a sob gathering like a great knot in her chest. This was not adventure. This was horrible.

She turned away and headed back for the camp. Then, *Boom!*

And that was the last thing she heard.

"A girl! Saints in Heaven, 'tis a girl!"

"Aye, yer right, man, 'tis a girl, for sure."

"Of course it's a girl. That's what I just said, booby. Be ye deaf?"

Meg opened her eyes and looked straight up. Three sets of eyes stared back down into hers—eyes that belonged to soldiers who were easing her onto a stretcher.

"Have a care, now ... gently, gently.... There! Mind that leg, man, 'tis cut bad. And swelled up nearly stiff ...

"Never ye mind, lassie, ever'thing's going to be all right. 'Tis a miracle, sure, yer alive ... blast like that ... but you'll live to tell the story.... 'Twould be a rare good story, too, I warrant, to hear how ye came to be here in the first place...."

Meg closed her eyes as the soldiers lifted the stretcher and carried her off the battlefield.

IV

Boulogne

W HEN Meg opened her eyes again, men lay on stretchers all about her, groaning, sleeping, talking quietly. The sharp smells of herbs and vinegar, of potions and poultices mingled in the close air of the room. Something felt tight around her head and across her forehead—not at all like her hat. She reached up . . . *bandages!* And then she remembered. There'd been an explosion . . . a shell or a cannonball. But after that everything was a blank.

Suddenly her hand slipped away from her head and caught in the strands of her hair. *Her hair!* Long and red-brown, it tumbled across her shoulders.

Meg looked around in a panic. Where was she? Not in a tent. This was a building. Sunlight filtered through its thatched roof in bright yellow slivers and streamed

through its windows in hard square patches. She tried to sit up. In pain she fell back again against her stretcher. Her bones ached, her muscles ached, her body felt like one great bruise. And there was a terrific throbbing in her left leg.

"Well, lass," said a man who hurried over when he saw Meg move, "I see you've come to a bit. And just in time for a fresh dressing on that bad leg of yours." And he set to work on Meg's leg, coating it with a foul-smelling paste from an earthenware pot and wrapping it round and round with a clean white cloth.

"Where am I?" asked Meg. "And who are you? And what happened? And what's become of the king and the army and the French and Boulogne?"

"Easy now, lass, don't get yourself overwrought," the man soothed. "I'm Roger Stillwell, physician to His Majesty's army. You've got your fair share of cuts and bruises and this leg here has had such a wrenching and twisting that 'tis likely all stretched and torn inside. But in a week or two, God willing, you'll be up and about and your leg as good as new."

"But where am I?" Meg asked again, her panic returning.

"Why, you're in a hospital. In Boulogne. Did you not know? 'Tis an English city now. The French put up a fierce fight, but with that great gaping hole in the wall they could never hold out against King Harry's mighty army." Roger Stillwell cut off a long length of bandage, and Meg leaned back with a sigh of relief. At least they had won. She shut her eyes at the awful memory of battle. Heaven only knew where she would have ended up if they had lost.

"But now 'tis my turn to ask a question or two," the physician resumed with a smile as he began to wrap again. "Just who might you be, mistress, and how came you to be with the army in France?"

So Meg told her story to the physician Roger Stillwell, and the soldier Greg Long became a part of her past. Once again she was quite simply Long Meg.

As the days passed, Meg's cuts and bruises healed and her leg mended. By the end of two weeks only a small limp remained from her injuries.

By the end of two weeks nothing remained of the gap in the wall of Boulogne. The king had ordered the walls rebuilt even stronger than before. And when he was sure that the city was safe, he took his main army and marched deeper into France, leaving a small company behind to guard the city.

Meg was left behind to help with the wounded. Not just English wounded, but French, too—left in the city by the fleeing soldiers and townspeople.

Meg was miserable. Her dreams of adventure had

turned out to be a nightmare. And here she was, stuck in a city in a foreign land—for no telling how long—doing just what she'd been doing at the inn. Waiting on people. And half of them she couldn't even understand when they complained about their ailments—their *douleurs* and their *blessures* and their *maux de tête*. Sometimes at night, when she'd finally finished changing all the dressings and put the fire out under the kettle, and when her leg started to ache and swell the way it always did when she'd been on it too long, she just sat down and sobbed.

But there was one thing she could be glad about. There was plenty of food. Toward the end of the siege, the army's supplies had begun to run out and she'd been hungry all the time. But the people of Boulogne had fled so suddenly they'd left their barns full of livestock and their storerooms bulging. Bags of flour and beans and barley leaned against barrels of pickled fish and salted pork. Strings of garlic and bunches of herbs hung from the rafters with links of dark and spicy sausages. And lining the shelves were the most delicious-smelling pots of jams and preserves marked *confiture.* Meg always felt a little bit better when she'd had something good to eat.

Another thing she couldn't complain about was the weather. The sun shone and the air was crisp with autumn. The countryside was so quiet and peaceful that the soldiers played at bowling on the green with their French prisoners and grew jolly on hearty French wines.

And it helped a lot, too, when soldiers who had seen her on the battlefield spoke of her courage and her skill with a sword.

"Stood her ground as brave as any knight, she did. Held off every Frenchman who came her way."

"I saw her take on two men at once. Disarmed them both before you could bat an eye."

"Hard to believe a girl could fight like that. Her sword flew so swift you could hardly see it!"

Word of Meg's feats spread through the company. Though she was a girl, she was admired and respected as a tried and tested soldier. Meg felt proud and her spirits began to rise.

Then one day, without any warning, a large French army came marching across the countryside. For ten days they fired their cannons at the walls. But it was no use. They could not recapture Boulogne.

They did not give up and go back to Paris, though. Instead, they spread out their camp and encircled the city.

" 'Tis a blockade they're planning," said one of the soldiers, a man who'd seen many campaigns. "Day and night the French will watch our gates. And as long as they are there, not you nor I nor any other soul can leave or enter Boulogne. 'Twill be hard times for us before long, I fear."

Meg's spirits sank. Would she ever see Westminster again?

Next day, the weather turned cold. Savage winds blew in from the sea, and heavy, gray sheets of rain swept across the city.

For weeks the foul weather continued. In the French camp the trenches turned into streams. Horses and soldiers bogged down in the mud. Still, they did not retreat. And they kept on watching the gates.

But things were even worse for the English inside the city. Just as the French had hoped, their food was running

" 'Tis not their cannonballs I fear, Meg," said the sentry, and he pointed into the distance.

Meg squinted up her eyes and looked out across the plain. Day was just about to break, and what she saw coming toward her through the pale mist of dawn made her heart skip a beat and her stomach turn a flip.

There were French soldiers, all right, but they were carrying ladders. And then Meg understood. They had carefully planned this attack. They had known that without food the English soldiers would get weak and sick. And somehow they knew that by now only a few men were well enough to fight—probably a prisoner had given them a sign. And they knew, too, just as Meg knew, that with hardly any English to worry about, the ladders would get them over the walls and into the city in no time.

Frantically she looked from one sentry to the other. "There must be something we can do!" she cried. But no one had an answer, and one by one they lowered their eyes and turned away.

As Meg watched the French soldiers moving toward the city, clustered together in little groups around the ladders, they reminded her of an army of ants she had once watched carrying off crusts of bread. But ants they weren't. They were the French. And soon they would be swarming into Boulogne! Desperately Meg turned and diers were quartered. She ran inside. The men were all in their beds.

"Get up, man!" she hissed as she shook one of the soldiers. But he only groaned and tossed a bit and then was still again.

"Wake up! Wake up!" She tried to rouse the man beside him. He opened his eyes and raised himself on an elbow, but fell back against his pillow, his brow wet with fever.

Meg tried another soldier, then another. Across the room a thin, pale man staggered to his feet and began to pull on his shirt. But one look at his gaunt face and trembling hands and Meg knew he couldn't help.

She looked around the room. It was no use trying to get the others up. They were all too weak and sick. She would have to see what she could do herself. And she ran to the wall to see what was going on.

"What is it?" she called to the sentry as she hurried up the steps to the top.

"The French," he replied. "They're getting ready to attack."

"Then let them," said Meg. "We have no cause for worry. Our men may be sick, but these thick, strong walls will keep them out and bounce their cannonballs right back to them."

" 'Tis not their cannonballs I fear, Meg," said the sentry, and he pointed into the distance.

Meg squinted up her eyes and looked out across the plain. Day was just about to break, and what she saw coming toward her through the pale mist of dawn made her heart skip a beat and her stomach turn a flip.

There were French soldiers, all right, but they were carrying ladders. And then Meg understood. They had carefully planned this attack. They had known that without food the English soldiers would get weak and sick. And somehow they knew that by now only a few men were well enough to fight—probably a prisoner had given them a sign. And they knew, too, just as Meg knew, that with hardly any English to worry about, the ladders would get them over the walls and into the city in no time.

Frantically she looked from one sentry to the other. "There must be something we can do!" she cried. But no one had an answer, and one by one they lowered their eyes and turned away.

As Meg watched the French soldiers moving toward the city, clustered together in little groups around the ladders, they reminded her of an army of ants she had once watched carrying off crusts of bread. But ants they weren't. They were the French. And soon they would be swarming into Boulogne! Desperately Meg turned and

Meg's spirits sank. Would she ever see Westminster again?

Next day, the weather turned cold. Savage winds blew in from the sea, and heavy, gray sheets of rain swept across the city.

For weeks the foul weather continued. In the French camp the trenches turned into streams. Horses and soldiers bogged down in the mud. Still, they did not retreat. And they kept on watching the gates.

But things were even worse for the English inside the city. Just as the French had hoped, their food was running

out. Weak from hunger, and cold and wet, the soldiers began to get sick. One after another they took to their beds, and Meg was busier than ever, cooling the feverish, warming the chilled, mixing ointments, potions, and plasters. But the soldiers got sick faster than they got well, and before long only a few men were left to defend the city.

Finally, one night, the rain stopped. The heavy clouds broke apart and went scudding over the horizon, leaving behind a skyful of stars.

"Perhaps the worst is over," sighed Meg and the soldiers on duty. And they went to bed with happier hearts.

But late that night, just before daylight, Meg suddenly opened her eyes. She'd heard something. Wide awake, not moving a muscle, she listened. Again the sound came, tearing through the stillness with unmistakable urgency. It was the bell, the alarm. Someone—the sentry, of course—was ringing it furiously, warning of an attack.

Meg jumped out of bed. She threw on her clothes and pulled on her boots. Then, grabbing up her sword, she headed for the wall.

But something was wrong. Her footsteps echoed in the silence as she ran through the empty street. Where were the others, she wondered.

Just ahead on the left was a house where English sol-

looked back across the sleeping city. How peaceful it was now, so still and dark and quiet.

But what was that? A light was shining from one of the houses. And huddled in front of the open door stood a group of women.

Meg recognized them at once. They were the washerwomen who had come with the army to France. Each morning they rose before dawn to begin the day's washing, and they, too, had heard the bell and come outside to see what the trouble was.

Suddenly, as they stood looking up at Meg, a great cloud of steam came pouring out of the door and billowed up around them. And at that moment Meg had an idea.

Quickly she counted the women. "One, two, three, four, five . . ." There were eleven outside the door, and more, she hoped, inside. Perhaps it would work. . . . But there was not a minute to lose.

Meg hurried down the steps and sped through the dark streets, gritting her teeth at the pain that shot up her left leg.

"Good women! Good women!" she called to the astonished laundresses. "The French are attacking the city, and all our soldiers are sick. But I have an idea, and perhaps *we* can save Boulogne. Come inside with me and I will tell you my plan."

The women followed Meg into the house. It was a single large room with several fireplaces. In each one steaming kettles of water hung bubbling over the fire. And on the long tables that took up most of the room, fat tubs of hot, soapy wash water sat waiting for the heaps and piles of sheets and shirts and breeches that lay scattered in between them.

Meg explained her plan, and the women quickly went to work. First they gathered up all the empty buckets they could find and filled them with the hot wash water from the tubs. And as soon as they had emptied a tub, they filled it again with the boiling water from the kettles, being careful to add great quantities of soap.

Then, each carrying a bucket of wash water in each hand, the women hurried after Meg to the city wall. And they got there just in time, for the French had raised their ladders, and on each one several soldiers were already on the way up.

Silently the women moved along the top of the wall and crouched behind the battlement. And beside each woman sat her two buckets of hot, soapy wash water.

Hardly daring to breathe, they waited without a sound while the *scrape, scrape* of the soldiers' boots on the ladders came closer and closer and closer. . . .

Then, from somewhere on the wall, a whistle cut

through the silence. And just as Meg had known they would, the startled men on the ladders jerked back their heads and looked up.

But they never saw a thing! For at that very moment each woman emptied her buckets, and each man received full in his face a tremendous gush of steaming hot wash water.

Splat! went the water, and down went the men. And the first man on each ladder knocked the second man off, and the two of them landed smack on the head of the third man, and so on down the ladders they tumbled, *plop, plop, plop,* like rows of falling dominoes, till they hit the ground below.

What a jumble and tumble of men there was then on the ground outside the wall. The soldiers lay in wriggling heaps of arms, legs, heads, bodies, and feet. And with their eyes full of soapsuds, they couldn't even see to get themselves untangled. Tears ran down their cheeks as they pushed and pulled and yanked and tugged, trying to get themselves free. But the problem was that in all the confusion no one could tell which leg was his, or which was his arm, or whose foot it was that had landed in his face.

Meanwhile, Meg and the washerwomen were busy up on the wall. As soon as the soldiers had fallen, they had dropped their buckets and gathered around the ladders.

Pulling and working together, they drew each one up over the wall and stowed it safely inside the city. By the time the French had rubbed the soap from their eyes and could see again, their ladders had disappeared.

Boulogne was saved. Without their ladders, the French would never be able to get inside the city. All they could do was untangle themselves and slink back down the hillside as Meg and the sentries and the washerwomen cheered and cried and threw their arms around each other.

"It worked! It worked!" the washerwomen cried. "It was your idea and it worked, Meg. You saved the city and you saved our lives."

"You're wrong," said Meg with a grin. " 'Twas my idea, that's so. But 'twas all of us working together that saved the city. And if I saved your lives, then you saved mine. I wouldn't have been worth a groat without you." Suddenly Meg's face went white and she collapsed right where she was standing.

"Meg! Long Meg, what is it?" the women gasped, patting her cheeks and fanning her face.

" 'Tis only this blasted leg," said Meg. "Still gives me trouble, you know. . . . Seems I overdid it a bit tonight," she added with a laugh as she tried to get up. But it was no use. Meg's leg refused to carry her another step, and the soldiers and washerwomen carried her down from the wall.

This was on a Wednesday. On Friday the French packed up and left posthaste for Paris. And on Saturday everyone found out why, for in the middle of the morning King Henry came galloping into the city with a host of knights and soldiers. During the attack, one of the English soldiers had slipped out of the gate and ridden full speed to fetch him, and when the French had learned he was coming, they'd cleared out fast.

"Take us at once to this girl called Long Meg," the king commanded when his men had helped him down from his horse. And he limped right into the room full of sick and wounded soldiers where Meg lay now, her swollen leg propped up on a pillow.

"Your Majesty!" Meg gasped, hardly believing her eyes.

"Well, mistress!" the king roared, his legs apart and his hands on his hips. "It has come to our ears how you have saved our city."

"Begging pardon, sire, 'tis—"

"Nay, Long Meg, we are much indebted to you," the king continued, raising a ring-covered hand to silence her, "and we mean to reward you for your brave act and your service to our crown." With these words he pulled out a small brown bag and emptied it. *Plink, plink, plink* . . . ten, twenty, thirty—more gold coins than Meg could count spilled into her lap.

Meg couldn't say a word, not even when one after the other more brown bags appeared, almost as big as the first. One for each of the washerwomen.

Suddenly the king bent over Meg's leg and studied it closely. "What ails your leg?" he asked, more like a father than a king.

And as Meg explained, he listened and stroked his beard. "Hmmm," he nodded, "hmmm.

"Our own leg is much given to swellings," he resumed when Meg had finished, lifting his own swollen leg for her to see, "especially after such a ride as we have had this morning. And on numerous occasions it troubles us with great pain. Therefore we have become expert at devising our own medicines, and we shall prescribe for you our own personal plaster for sore legs." And calling for ink and quill, King Henry VIII of England wrote out this recipe for Meg:

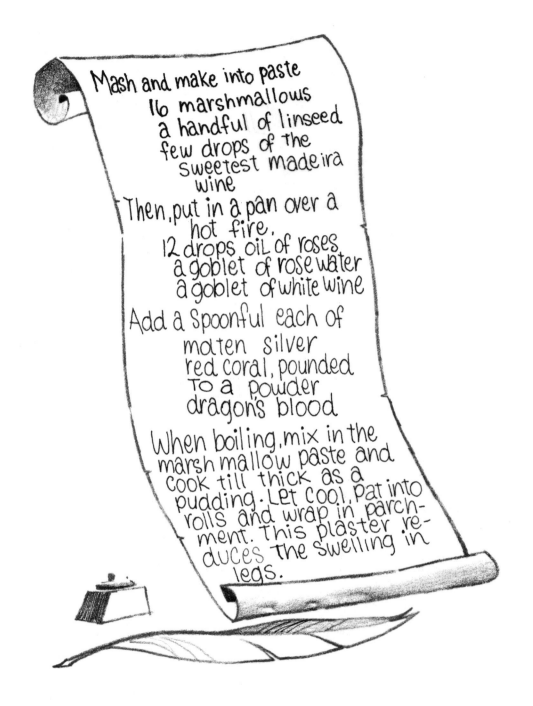

Mash and make into paste
  16 marshmallows
  a handful of linseed
  few drops of the
    sweetest madeira
    wine
Then, put in a pan over a
    hot fire,
  12 drops oil of roses
  a goblet of rose water
  a goblet of white wine

Add a spoonful each of
  molten silver
  red coral, pounded
  to a powder
  dragon's blood

When boiling, mix in the
marshmallow paste and
cook till thick as a
pudding. Let cool, pat into
rolls and wrap in parch-
ment. This plaster re-
duces the swelling in
legs.

Well, Meg's leg did get better, though whether the king's plaster actually helped or not, it's hard to say. But there is one thing that can be said for certain. The king's gold helped a lot. The washerwomen didn't have to wash anymore. And Meg never had to work at an inn again. With all that gold she was able to spend the rest of her life doing what she still wanted to do. And that was to have adventures.

Author's Note

The stories about Long Meg are very old. In fact, no one knows just how or when they got started. Probably, like most legends, they were passed around from person to person for many years before they were ever written down.

The first book we have of Long Meg's "mad merry pranks" was printed in 1620, nearly four hundred years ago. There are eighteen chapters, or stories, and the story you have just read is based on two of them.

In the introduction to the stories, the author compares Meg to another popular legendary character of the time, Robin Hood. The comparison is a fair one, I think, for, like Robin Hood, Meg is a strong and skillful fighter. She is as generous and good-hearted as she is strong, always using her sword and her wits to defend the poor and the unfortunate, and she has no use at all for persons who are phony or pompous.

Scholars have argued for years about whether or not Long Meg was a real person. Yet today, just as with Robin Hood, the mystery remains unsolved.

If you're the kind of person who loves a mystery, and if you should ever get to London, you might want to do a little investigation of your own. If so, you should begin at Westminster Abbey, a very old and beautiful church. There among the tombs of kings and queens and monks and abbots you will see an enormous slab of blue marble. Your guide will tell you that it is called "Long Meg of Westminster" and that no one knows who lies below it. Some say it marks the grave of twenty-six monks who died in the Great Plague of London and were buried all together. But there are others who believe it marks the grave of a woman who lived long ago and was as tall and as strong as a man, who went away to France and saved the city of Boulogne for King Henry VIII, and, most important of all, who was called Long Meg of Westminster.

Whatever the truth about Long Meg's existence, many scholars have agreed that a woman (or perhaps several women) *like* Meg did really live and that the stories we have today grew out of her (or their) deeds.

In writing *Long Meg* I am especially grateful to my friend Julia Wolf Mazow, who told me about the original stories, and to my editor, Dinah Stevenson, who believed in the book and whose excellent suggestions inspired and challenged me. Historical and background details came from a number of sources; particularly valuable to me, however, was Carolly Erickson's excellent biography, *Great Harry: The Extravagant Life of Henry VIII* (Summit Books, 1980).

ROSEMARY MINARD was raised in Conroe, Texas. She graduated from Sophie Newcomb College of Tulane University and received a master's degree from the University of Houston. She lived in Belgium for several years, has traveled throughout Europe, and has visited the People's Republic of China. Ms. Minard is the author of *Womenfolk and Fairy Tales.* She is the co-owner of a writing, editing, and research firm, and lives in Houston with her husband and their two sons.

PHILIP SMITH grew up in the San Francisco Bay Area. He held a variety of jobs, and after serving in the army attended the California College of Arts and Crafts in Oakland. He worked as a studio artist and as art director for advertising agencies before deciding to devote full time to freelance illustration. Mr. Smith has one grown daughter and lives in Sonoma, California, where he enjoys the ocean, riding his bike, going to foreign films, and inventing things.